Dear Parent:

Congratulations! Your child is taking the first steps on an exciting journey. The destination? Independent reading!

STEP INTO READING® will help your child get there. The program offers five steps to reading success. Each step includes fun stories and colorful art. There are also Step into Reading Sticker Books, Step into Reading Math Readers, Step into Reading Phonics Readers, Step into Reading Write-In Readers, and Step into Reading Phonics Boxed Sets—a complete literacy program with something for every child.

Learning to Read, Step by Step!

Ready to Read   Preschool–Kindergarten
• big type and easy words • rhyme and rhythm • picture clues
For children who know the alphabet and are eager to begin reading.

Reading with Help   Preschool–Grade 1
• basic vocabulary • short sentences • simple stories
For children who recognize familiar words and sound out new words with help.

Reading on Your Own   Grades 1–3
• engaging characters • easy-to-follow plots • popular topics
For children who are ready to read on their own.

Reading Paragraphs   Grades 2–3
• challenging vocabulary • short paragraphs • exciting stories
For newly independent readers who read simple sentences with confidence.

Ready for Chapters   Grades 2–4
• chapters • longer paragraphs • full-color art
For children who want to take the plunge into chapter books but still like colorful pictures.

STEP INTO READING® is designed to give every child a successful reading experience. The grade levels are only guides. Children can progress through the steps at their own speed, developing confidence in their reading, no matter what their grade.

Remember, a lifetime love of reading starts with a single step!

created by

[signature: Stephen Hillenburg]

Visit us on the Web!
StepIntoReading.com
randomhouse.com/kids

Educators and librarians, for a variety of teaching tools, visit us at RHTeachersLibrarians.com

ISBN: 978-0-385-37608-2 (trade) — ISBN: 978-0-385-37609-9 (lib. bdg.)
Printed in the United States of America   10 9 8 7 6 5 4 3 2 1

STEP INTO READING®

STEP 2

nickelodeon

SpongeBob SQUAREPANTS

Show Me the Bunny!

By Steven Banks

Cover illustrated by Fabrizio Petrossi

Interior illustrated by
C. H. Greenblatt and William Reiss

Random House 🏠 New York

It is Easter.

Patrick decorates his house
with blinking lights.

"Um, the Easter Bunny
is coming,
not Santa Claus,"
says SpongeBob.

That night,
the Easter Bunny visits
Patrick's house.

Patrick thinks
the Easter Bunny
is a monster.
He scares
the Easter Bunny away.

Honk!

"It's Easter morning!"
SpongeBob shouts.

Patrick tells SpongeBob
how he stopped the monster.
"That was the Easter Bunny!"
says SpongeBob.

"I've ruined Easter!"
cries Patrick.

"I will fix

Patrick's Easter,"

says SpongeBob.

He paints eggs.

SpongeBob finds

his Easter Bunny costume.

SpongeBob will be
the Easter Bunny.
He hides eggs
for Patrick to find.

The Easter Bunny
visits Patrick.
"Merry Easter!"
shouts Patrick.

The Easter Bunny
tells Patrick about
the hidden eggs.
Patrick is excited
to start the egg hunt.

SpongeBob changes
out of his costume.
Patrick arrives
for the hunt.

The egg hunt begins!

Patrick eats
all of his eggs!

SpongeBob feels bad
for Patrick.
He gives Patrick
his eggs.

"We have no eggs, Gary!"
cries SpongeBob.
Then Patrick
feels bad.

Patrick gives SpongeBob
the biggest egg
in Bikini Bottom.

The egg starts
to shake and crack!

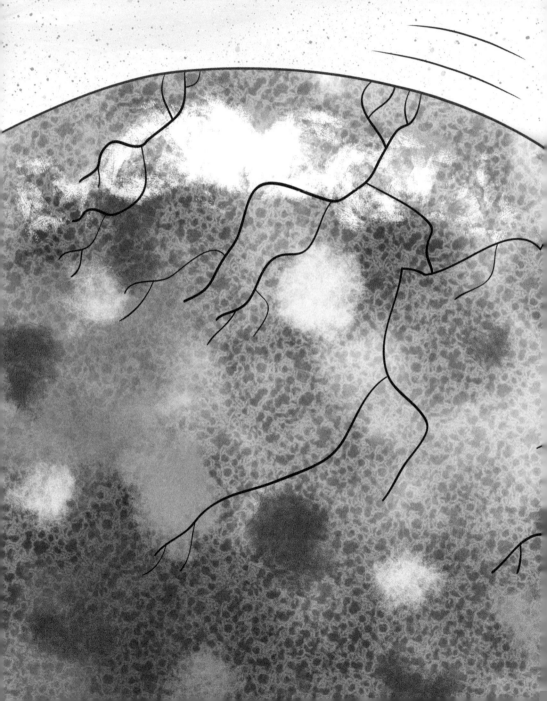

"That is not
an Easter Egg,"
SpongeBob says.

The egg hatches.

A giant fish is inside!

"The Easter Fish is here!"

yells Patrick.